The Harmon's

Christmas Time
By Gail Gibbons

Holiday House · New York

To Nancy and Jim White

Library of Congress Cataloging
in Publication Data

Gibbons, Gail.
Christmas time.

Summary: A brief look at why and
how we celebrate Christmas.
1. Christmas—Juvenile literature.
[1. Christmas] I. Title.
GT4985.G44   394.2'68282   82-1038
ISBN 0-8234-0453-6   AACR2
ISBN 0-8234-0575-3 (pbk.)

DECEMBER 25

CHRISTMAS is on December 25th. On that day the birth of Jesus Christ is celebrated.

He was born many years ago in a stable in Bethlehem. His parents, Mary and Joseph, had to sleep in the stable, because they were away from home and couldn't find room in an inn.

An angel told three shepherds about the Christ Child's birth, and they went to Bethlehem to see Him.

There were also three wise men who journeyed to the stable. They followed a bright star that appeared in the sky over Bethlehem.

They brought Jesus gifts and worshiped Him.

They believed He was the Son of God.

Before Christmas Day, some homes are decorated with evergreens.

Unlike other trees, an evergreen stays green all year.

It is thought of as the "tree of life." It gives the feeling of hope.

Some people pick out an evergreen tree . . .

and bring it home to decorate.

They string lights on the tree. The lights look like the stars of the heavens.

They put candles in their windows, and decorate their homes with lights. The Christmas lights are to remind people of the light Christ brought into the world when He was born.

Ornaments are hung on a Christmas tree.

Sometimes a star is placed at the top to remind us of the star of Bethlehem.

The Christmas season is also a time for singing carols.

On Christmas Eve or on Christmas Day, some people go to church to hear the story of the Christ Child's birth. They pray. Sometimes the church has many candles.

Christmas hymns are sung.

Christmas is a time of gift giving to show love for others.
The three wise men brought their gifts to the Christ Child.

Santa Claus brings gifts, too. He is also called Saint Nicholas.
Many years ago, Dutch children called him Sinterklaas.
In America, the name slowly changed to Santa Claus.

Saint Nicholas lived a long time ago. He loved giving gifts
and helping people. He was made a saint because he was
loved so much.

It is said that Saint Nicholas threw three bags of gold down a chimney for three poor girls. One of the bags landed in a stocking hung by the chimney to dry.

Perhaps that is why stockings are hung for Santa to fill, and
why some think Santa slides down chimneys.

Santa Claus is jolly and kind. He lives at the North Pole. All year long he is busy making gifts.

On Christmas Eve he gets into his sleigh, and is pulled
through the starry skies by his reindeer.

He enters many homes, stuffs stockings, and leaves gifts
under the Christmas trees.

Christmas Day is a time for presents . . .

and families . . .

and for enjoying a tasty meal.

Christmas Day is a time for love, joy and peace.